Franklin and the New Teacher

From a direct-to-video special, a Nelvana Limited
production, produced with the participation of
The Family Channel Inc. and based on the Franklin
books by Paulette Bourgeois and Brenda Clark.

Nelvana is a registered trademark of Nelvana Limited.
Corus is a trademark of Corus Entertainment Inc.

TV tie-in adaptation written by Sharon Jennings
and illustrated by Céleste Gagnon, Sasha McIntyre,
Alice Sinkner, Jelena Sisic and Shelley Southern

Based on the direct-to-video special
Back to School with Franklin © 2003
Nelvana Limited, written by John van Bruggen.

Kids Can Press acknowledges the financial support of the Government of
Ontario, through the Ontario Media Development Corporation's Ontario Book
Initiative; the Ontario Arts Council; the Canada Council for the Arts; and the
Government of Canada, through the BPIDP, for our publishing activity.

Published in Canada by
Kids Can Press Ltd.
29 Birch Avenue
Toronto, ON M4V 1E2

Published in the U.S. by
Kids Can Press Ltd.
2250 Military Road
Tonawanda, NY 14150

www.kidscanpress.com

Series editor: Tara Walker
Edited by Jennifer Stokes

Printed and bound in China by WKT Company Limited

This book is smyth sewn casebound.

CM 04 0 9 8 7 6 5 4 3 2 1

National Library of Canada Cataloguing in Publication Data

Jennings, Sharon
     Franklin and the new teacher / Sharon Jennings ; illustrated by Céleste
Gagnon ... [et al.].

(A Franklin TV storybook.)
The character Franklin was created by Paulette Bourgeois and Brenda Clark.
ISBN 1-55337-499-1 (bound).

I. Gagnon, Céleste II. Bourgeois, Paulette III. Clark, Brenda IV. Title.
V. Series: Franklin TV storybook.

PS8569.E563F7172 2004   jC813'.54   C2003-907128-6

Kids Can Press is a *Corus*™ Entertainment company

Franklin and the New Teacher

Kids Can Press

FRANKLIN had always lived in the same
house in the same town. Every day he took the
same bus to the same school, and his teacher was
Mr. Owl. Franklin liked things to stay the same.
Then came the start of the new school year,
and things were a little different.

At the end of summer holidays, Mr. Owl broke his foot. A supply teacher was coming to take his place. Franklin was worried.

"I want Mr. Owl to be my teacher," he told his parents.

Then he had an idea.

"I think I'll wait for Mr. Owl to come back," he said.

Franklin's parents smiled.

"You'll be fine," his mother replied.

On the first day of school, Franklin moaned and groaned and rubbed his tummy.

"Hmmm," said his mother. "Maybe you have a case of new-teacheritis."

Franklin nodded.

"I'd better stay home," he replied.

His mother gave him a hug.

"You'll feel better as soon as you're with your friends," she said.

Franklin's mother was wrong. All of Franklin's friends were worried, too.

"What if he's big and scary?" asked Snail.

"What if he won't let us have snack time?" asked Bear.

"What if he gives us too much work?" asked Rabbit.

Everyone was quiet as the bus pulled into the schoolyard.

At nine o'clock, the new teacher stepped outside and rang the bell.

"G'day!" she hollered. "My name is Ms. Koala."

Everyone was surprised.

"He's a *she*," whispered Franklin.

The students filed into the classroom.

"You may sit wherever you like," said Ms. Koala.

Beaver put up her hand.

"Franklin and Bear shouldn't sit together,"
she said. "They talk too much."

"But mates want to sit together," replied Ms. Koala.
"Fair dinkum! School should be fun."

Franklin hurried to sit beside Bear.

"Why does she talk funny?" whispered Bear.

"Because she's not Mr. Owl. That's why,"
Franklin answered.

Ms. Koala handed out paper and books,
pencils and rulers.

"Mr. Owl has left lots of work for us," she said.
Then she sighed. "What a ripper day to be stuck inside.
When I left Down Under, it was winter."

"Huh?" said Franklin.

Ms. Koala smiled.

"Oz," she said. "You know."

But Franklin didn't know. Neither did anyone else.

Ms. Koala pointed to the classroom globe.

"I'm from Australia," she explained. "See, class? Australia's 'down under' from where we are now. We have winter when you have summer."

"Why did you leave Australia?" Franklin asked.

"I like to try new things," Ms. Koala answered.

Franklin thought about the same cereal he always ate for breakfast and the same lunch he brought to school every day. Then he thought about Mr. Owl.

"I don't," he said. He glared at Ms. Koala. "I like everything to stay the same."

"Hmmm," said Ms. Koala.

At recess, Ms. Koala followed Franklin outside.

"I need your help, mate," she told him. "I think some of the others miss Mr. Owl."

Franklin nodded.

"They probably think I'm different," she added, "and that I talk funny."

Franklin nodded again.

Ms. Koala continued. "Maybe if they got to know me a bit better, they wouldn't worry so much. Any ideas, mate?"

Franklin shook his head. Ms. Koala sighed.

In a little while, Ms. Koala rang the bell.
When everyone was in line, she held up a curved
piece of polished wood.

"Let's stay outside a bit longer," she said.
"And I'll show you how to use a boomerang."

She led the class to the field.

"When you throw a boomerang just right, it
circles around and comes back to you. Like this."
Ms. Koala flicked her wrist.

"Wow!" everyone exclaimed.

The whole class wanted to try. And they did,
over and over and over.

"It's not as easy as it looks," grumbled Beaver.

Soon, it was Franklin's turn again. He hoped he could do it. Maybe he could show Mr. Owl when he got back. He held his arm up and out to the side and let go.

He watched the boomerang sail out across the field. Then he stared in amazement as the boomerang swung back.

"Good onya, Franklin!" cried Ms. Koala. "You're a true blue Aussie now!"

Franklin frowned.

"I am?" he asked.

Back in the classroom, Ms. Koala said it was time for Show and Tell.

"Mr. Owl says we're too big for Show and Tell," said Snail.

"So we didn't bring anything," added Franklin.

"Too bad," said Ms. Koala. "Show and Tell is a good way to get to know people. Well, let's do some math instead."

She started writing on the board.

Franklin sat thinking.

Slowly, he put up his hand.

Ms. Koala turned around.

"Yes, Franklin?" she asked.

"I was wondering if you could be Show and Tell," he said. "You could tell us all about Australia."

"Bonzer, Franklin!" exclaimed Ms. Koala. "What a great idea."

Franklin grinned.

For the rest of the morning, Ms. Koala talked about Australia. She showed the class photos of her family and friends. She found a book in the library and showed them pictures of all kinds of things they'd never seen before.

"Do you like Australia?" asked Franklin.

"Fair dinkum!" she answered. "Too right!"

That night over supper, Franklin's parents asked if he liked the new teacher.

"Ms. Koala?" said Franklin. "Fair dinkum! She's from Oz. You know, Down Under."

His parents laughed.

"And what about Mr. Owl?" asked his mother. "Do you miss him?"

Franklin stopped to think.

"A little bit," he said. "But it's okay. I know he'll be back."

Then Franklin laughed.
"Just like a boomerang!"